W9-CBS-942

PIGAROONS

ARTHUR GEISERT

HOUGHTON MIFFLIN COMPANY BOSTON 2004

Walter Lorraine Books

For Bonnie

Walter Lorraine (wr) Books

Copyright © 2004 by Arthur Geisert

All rights reserved. For information about permission
to reproduce selections from this book, write to Permissions,
Houghton Mifflin Company, 215 Park Avenue South,
New York, New York 10003.

www.houghtonmifflinbooks.com

Library of Congress Cataloging-in-Publication Data

Geisert, Arthur.
  Pigaroons / Arthur Geisert.
       p. cm.
  "Walter Lorraine Books."
  Summary: The River Patrollers are tired of the Pigaroons always stealing things,
so when they steal a block of ice and carve it for the annual ice festival, the River
Patrollers find an ingenious way to fight back.
    ISBN 0-618-41058-9 (hardcover)
  [1. Pigs—Fiction. 2. Stealing—Fiction. 3. Festivals—Fiction.] I. Title.
   PZ7.G2724Pd 2004
   [E]—dc22
                                                                    2004000574

ISBN–13: 978-0-618-41058-3

Printed in Mexico
10 9 8 7 6 5 4 3 2 1

The River Patrollers lived in a stone quarry on Porcine Ridge overlooking the river. There was a small pond of pure water in the quarry. Every year they cut one big block of crystal-clear ice from the pond and carved a sculpture for the Ice Festival. The River Patrollers were skilled ice sculptors, and they usually won first prize.

Across the river on Spanish Ridge lived descendants of Spanish pirates. They were called "Pigaroons," and, true to their heritage, they stole stuff.

One night, while the River Patrollers slept,

the Pigaroons stole their annual block of ice.

They took the ice back to Spanish Ridge. They, too, knew how to carve ice sculpture.

How clever they thought they were to take their rival's only
block of ice. Now they could win first prize at the Ice Festival.

At Spanish Ridge, near the houses made of logs stolen decades
before from the great rafts that floated down the Mississippi,

the Pigaroons got the block of ice ready for carving.

They quickly carved out a likeness of Hernando de Soto,
the famous Spanish explorer.

They also made popcorn balls to sell at the festival.

Across the river, the River Patrollers could see their
block of ice being carved.

One patriarch declared, "No more! They've stolen enough
stuff from us!" A plan was made.

On Ice Festival day, the Pigaroons loaded their popcorn balls and

the sculpture of Hernando de Soto and headed off to the Ice Festival.

On Porcine Ridge, the River Patrollers worked on their plan
to thwart the Pigaroons.

There was just enough ice left to cut one thin slab.
They worked and polished the ice until they were ready to go.

They loaded their flying machine and prepared it for flight.

At the festival, there was great fun and gaiety.

The Pigaroons' popcorn balls sold briskly. It looked as if
Hernando de Soto was a sure bet for first prize.

Luckily, flying conditions were in the River Patrollers' favor,
and they were on their way.

As they approached the Ice Festival, they adjusted their polished
piece of ice.

They focused it carefully on the Pigaroons' sculpture,

and Hernando de Soto began to melt.

Everyone gasped and stood stunned as Hernando disappeared.

When it was time for the judging, there was nothing there
to judge.

While they were at it, the River Patrollers focused their ice
lens on the popcorn balls and stuck them together.

Then they burned a giant portrait of Hernando de Soto into the snow,
which delighted everyone, except the Pigaroons, of course.

The River Patrollers were awarded first prize for their cleverness.
The Pigaroons were chastised and told never to steal again.
Not that that would ever do any good.